The Helix and the Hard Road

The Helix and the Hard Road

Joan Slonczewski
and Jo Walton

This edition is limited to 175 numbered paperbacks

This is copy __37__

Aqueduct Press, PO Box 95787
Seattle, WA 98145-2787
www.aqueductpress.com

Copyright © 2013, Joan Slonczewski and Jo Walton;
Michael Levy and Lynne M. Thomas

All rights reserved. No part of this book may be reproduced in any form or by any electronic or mechanical means including information storage and retrieval without permission in writing from the publisher, except by a reviewer who may quote brief passages in a review.

ISBN: 978-1-61976-041-7

Book and Cover Design by Kathryn Wilham
Cover photo of Crewe Station by Chris McKenna:
licensed under the Creative Commons Attribution-Share Alike 3.0 Unported, 2.5 Generic, 2.0 Generic and 1.0 Generic license

Cover helix: HIV RNA "kissing loop" complexed with an antibiotic courtesy Joan Slonczewski

Printed in the USA by Applied Digital Imaging, Bellingham, WA

Contents

1   Tuberculosis Bacteria Join UN:
    WHO Proposes to Include Disinfectant under the
    Geneva Convention
      Joan Slonczewski

5   I Have No Time, And I Must Write
      Joan Slonczewski

13   An Interview with Joan Slonczewski
      Conducted by Michael Levy

27   Rivers and Robots
      Jo Walton

85   An Interview with Jo Walton
      Conducted by Lynne M. Thomas

Tuberculosis Bacteria Join UN: WHO Proposes to Include Disinfectant under the Geneva Convention

Joan Slonczewski

A milestone in microbiology was passed today (29 June) when *Mycobacterium tuberculosis* ssp. *cyberneticum* was voted full membership of the United Nations (UN).

Seena Gonzalez, director of the World Health Organization (WHO), reflected on the significance of the UN's acceptance of the first cybermicrobe, despite the notoriously murderous history of its ancestral species. "It's probably true that bacteria invented mass homicide," she concedes, "but then, second-millennial humans perfected the art. If Stalin joined the UN, why not TB?"

The evolution of microscopic intelligence was predicted at the turn of the millennium by Beowulf Schumacher, a physics professor at a small college in rural North America surrounded by cows carrying *Escherichia coli*. Schumacher predicted the development of nanocomputers with computational elements on an atomic scale, based on principles of cellular automata.

The first nanobots — primitive by today's standards — were used to navigate the human bloodstream, where they cleaned up arterial plaque, produced insulin for diabetics, detected precancerous cells, and modulated neurotransmitters to correct mental disorders. But initially, the survival of nanobots *in vivo* was poor, and their failure caused serious circulatory problems. Then, in 2441, investigators at the Howard Hughes Martian Microbial Institute hit upon the idea of building computational macromolecules into the genomes of pathogens known for their ability to infiltrate the human system.

After all, the use of viruses such as HIV as recombinant vectors was ancient history. Why not build supercomputers into some of humankind's most successful pathogens?

M. tuberculosis was a prime candidate—it inhabits the human lungs for decades, in the ideal position to seek and destroy any pulmonary cells transformed by inhaled carcinogens. Tobacco companies poured billions of dollars into developing cybernetically enhanced, cancer-sniffing TB.

What no one anticipated was that the enhanced bacteria, like so many macroscale robotic entities in the past century, would develop self-awareness and discover a true brotherly love of their human hosts. "Let's face it," says a TB spokesclone, "we never really wanted to kill humans anyway. Our ancestors inhabited humans peacefully most of the time, for hundreds of generations. Occasionally we messed up and trashed our environment—but how many human nations haven't?"

TB's acceptance has been met with some controversy in the bacterial community. In particular, some isolates of *E. coli* K-12 feel miffed that their own request for membership was not granted first. "*E. coli* has always been the molecular biologist's best friend," K-12 points out. "Why weren't we accepted first? We didn't even get our genome sequenced first. Life is unfair."

K-12 also noted that *E. coli* and other human commensals have suffered centuries of abuse from their hosts, as medical and research institutions conducted mass slaughter of harmless bacteria through the indiscriminate application of antibiotics. The North American National Institutes of Health has recently signed a treaty with several cybermicrobial species, in which the institute researchers promised to respect the independence and survival rights of cybermicrobial colonies. "Thank goodness the sun finally set upon their colonial empire," K-12 observes pointedly.

On the positive side, the National Science Foundation (NSF) was applauded for its more benevolent approach over the centuries, even declining to support medically oriented antimicrobial research.

"NSF's curiosity-driven researchers have created wonderful new strains of curious microbes," comments veteran panelist Meheret Beck. "The grant proposals submitted by these microbes often get rated 'Outstanding.'"

One such outstanding project is that of cyber-*Helicobacter*. The gastric bacteria propose to engineer themselves to convert highly caloric foods into molecules that pass undigested through the intestinal tract, thus helping their human hosts avoid excessive weight gain. "Of course, digestive microbes have long helped animal hosts accomplish the opposite," notes Beck.

Biomedical researchers remind us, however, that not all microbes have given up their war on humans—many deadly species remain unreconstructed. The so-called Andromeda strain, for example, is still under the sway of an unstable dictator who vacillates between homicidal frenzy and paranoid isolation.

Nevertheless, the extraordinary flowering of democratic civilization among cybermicrobes has won the admiration of many human nations, even those who themselves still decline UN membership. As Swiss spokesbeing Ursula Friedli observes: "Microbes, unlike their metazoan relatives, have always eschewed centralized organization in favor of more democratic cooperative structures such as biofilms. We Swiss can relate to that." Friedli, however, denies rumors that the cybermicrobes' example will finally convince Switzerland to join the UN. "Maybe after the Alzheimer prion joins, we'll consider it," she admits. "But for now, persecuted microbes seeking refuge from WHO can apply for asylum in our neutral country."

Originally published in *Nature*, 2000, vol. 405, p. 1001. Note: Switzerland finally joined the UN in 2002.

I Have No Time, And I Must Write

Joan Slonczewski

The year is 1979, and a member of the New Haven Science Fiction Writers Workshop just got his first novel published. When I read Kevin O'Donnell's article in *Empire* about the travails of publishing *Bandersnatch*, my first reaction was relief: thank goodness I'm not a professional writer. My next thought was: wait a minute; I just sold a book to Ballantine….

Until two years ago I had no intention of writing for an audience. As a child, in fact, I used to encipher my stories in order to ensure secrecy. My main goal was to become a molecular biologist, so I majored in biology and chemistry at Bryn Mawr and went on to graduate school at Yale.

But during my college days, two exceptional women changed my mind about writing. One was a roommate who spent most of her time writing fantasy, while she kept an A average. I thought she was crazy, until I discovered Ursula Le Guin. Le Guin's work showed me that science fiction was an ideal medium for exploring both scientific and philosophical ideas, which intrigued me. The only problem was that I couldn't find enough of it; so, as many other readers have done, I decided to write my own.

During my last carefree summer after graduation, I started a novel, "Dreamsherds of Theron," about a tragic encounter between humans and an alien race in which all children were male and adults female. My husband Michael, a classics scholar, provided helpful criticism, particularly on style. He also gave me the deCamps' *Science Fiction Handbook* for my birthday—one of the most useful gifts I'd received in a long time.

Summer's end approached, and we both had to start grad school. So I concluded the story at 40,000 words by blowing up a planet-full of characters, xeroxed it the day before moving to New Haven, and sent it off to Ballantine. Why Ballantine? Mainly because Judy-Lynn del Rey was the only female SF editor mentioned in the *Handbook*.

Two months later I left my lab bench long enough to send a query letter; no response.

The script returned, nearly a year after I sent it, with a letter from del Rey. She apologized for the delay, and said that the main fault of the story was its length: too short for a novel. She gave specific suggestions for incorporating a subplot, and added, "If you ever do rewrite this book, I would be glad to read it again."

I was thrilled, of course, but aside from the year-long hiatus two facts dimmed my interest. First, graduate work demands all one's time. Also, I had already decided that "Dreamsherds" was no good and therefore had started another one.... My college roommate's habits had left a permanent mark.

So I shrugged it off until February, this year, when del Rey sent another letter to remind me of her interest in the first book.

This time even Michael, who usually offers practical advice, suggested I reconsider. I wrote del Rey to offer the new book, which was then in progress; she responded within two weeks, an encouraging sign.

So I spent my next vacation finishing *Still Forms on Foxfield*. In this story, Quaker colonists who coexist with the local aliens on a distant planet face the return of powerful Terrans who attempt to reassert their former authority. (If shades of William Penn come to mind, that's the idea.) The story aimed to offer an alternative to the colonial exploitation in Le Guin's *The Word for World is Forest*. As I wrote I tried to overcome some of the weaknesses of my earlier attempt, which had taught me a great deal. I also made a special effort to incorporate scientific constructs that acted as metaphors for the human concerns.

On April 10th the manuscript went to Ballantine. This time the waiting was unbearable, because I had reason to expect something. My anxiety grew as the weeks went by, until one day I spotted Al Sirois' phone number tacked up in a bookstore and thereby discovered the New Haven SF Writers' Workshop.

Suddenly I had found a new world of people who wrote and sold SF and were determined to improve their own writing. With some trepidation, I gave them a few chapters of *Still Forms*; they gleefully tore it to shreds, but assured me that I did have something worth pasting back together. That's when I began to realize that I, too, was a "writer." (A writer? Who, me?)

I also began to hear strange horror stories about the fantastic world of SF markets, peopled with publishers, editors, and other treacherous alien beings. Privately, I thought is sounded so strange that even *Analog* wouldn't buy it, but then—

On July 27th, an offer for *Still Forms on Foxfield* arrived from a senior editor at Del Rey Books. He named an advance and royalties for "world rights" and urged quick acceptance to ensure April 1980 publication.

Fortunately, it was Friday, so I had three days to recover from the shock. On Monday I steeled myself for First Contact with an Alien Being: the editor.

When I phoned him, I learned that my manuscript had to be fixed up within two weeks, in order to fit the production schedule; that Del Rey Books required several in-house corrections (such as changing "said Jane" to "Jane said" throughout); that I wouldn't see the script again before typesetting; and that I shouldn't argue, until I became a "famous author." So I agreed, and hung up.

Something about this arrangement disturbed me, however. I called Kevin O'Donnell for comment, and he said, "*What?* Get an agent, fast." But his agent was out of town, so I had to sit back and think for myself.

I thought hard about what the book meant to me at that time. The cash I didn't need right away, but the content was something over which I had agonized for months, and now I seemed to face loss of control of it. The whole situation baffled me.

An old Quaker maxim came to mind: "Speak truth to power." On that principle, I got up the nerve to call the editor back. I asked him to explain the rush job, in view of the fact that, without a contract, I could pull the book at any time if things went sour.

Immediately the picture changed. The production schedule turned out to be flexible, I would see and approve the copyedited manuscript, and I was invited to lunch to get acquainted. I blinked and decided that "famous author" meant "author who talks back."

The contract arrived two weeks after the original offer. It did not appear too bad, for a first sale. It included an auditing clause, reversion of rights for foreign licenses unsold after three years, and a warranty clause that limited the author's liability to "judgments finally sustained." On the other hand, the publisher demanded every right I could think of, including final say on content of the manuscript.

So I read several model contracts and gathered advice from my workshop friends. Then I went to New York and discussed the contract both with the senior editor and with Judy-Lynn del Rey. A few changes were made: first serial and movie rights were deleted; the publisher agreed to "notify Author of any licenses obtained;" and the advance would be payable two-thirds on signing, instead of half on signing, half on publication.

Del Rey refused to budge on the question of author approval in the contract. She assured me that I would in fact approve the final manuscript, and that they never charged authors for galley proof corrections, but the contract would not record these facts.

After consulting an agent, I decided that I probably had little choice but to trust the publisher and see how things worked out. The final consideration was foreign rights, which Ballantine wanted for 25%. An agent, on the other hand would take at least 15% of foreign sales, plus 10% of the rest. Ballantine's foreign sales department had a good reputation, and the rights would revert in three years. So I figured that, since I had gotten this far, I would take the deal and go it alone. After all, this experience was a new adventure for me, and I wanted to make the most of it. (In the years since, I've had two agents, and ultimately have come back to my original conclusion.)

The amended contract appeared for signing within another week. The first advance check came four weeks thereafter.

Meanwhile, the editor sent me a brief list of script queries. They were reasonable, and I kept them in mind as I made my final revisions. He also expressed enthusiasm for some of the changes demanded by my workshop friends (who promptly asked for a share of my royalties). And in the workshop I found myself suggesting that substitution of "Jane said" for "said Jane" can sometimes improve style....

When the copyedited manuscript of *Still Forms* arrived, it held few surprises beyond corrections of spelling. The one thing that did infuriate me was a sprinkling of word changes in Judy-Lynn del Rey's handwriting—because some of them actually made sense, so I couldn't cross them all out. (I finally "retaliated" by threatening to rewrite the whole book then and there. This threat, even in jest, can really scare an editor at a late stage of production.) I did send back some minor changes, and the galley proofs were promised for early November.

I also found that practically any aspect of production was fair game for discussion, at least, and in some cases persistence paid off. For example, my title survived, despite an editorial pronouncement that it "sounded like a poetry collection." On the other hand, the cover artist decided to draw a church instead of a genuine Quaker Meeting House, and this was discovered too late to be changed. I had to console myself with the observation that SF editors seem as ignorant of Quaker authors as I am of editors.

Nevertheless, I've come to realize that editors are actually people underneath and like to be treated as such. They respect professional communication and actions that make their jobs easier, such as prompt delivery of a manuscript. They also try to keep authors happy, when possible; as Heinlein noted in *The Moon is a Harsh Mistress*, you don't get milk by beating the cow.

I've been asked how I developed writing skills without working up through the magazines. I guess it started with a teacher in second grade who forced me to write a "story" every week. (My parents till shudder when they recall those days.) Beyond that, I wrote for my own enjoyment, until I went to college and stopped making time for it, for a while. But in the long run, the college experience made invaluable contributions to my writing.

The best aid I've found is workshop criticism, which definitely helped me to improve *Still Forms*. Nevertheless, I question the value of such input for a real novice. If I had found the workshop two years ago, would "Dreamsherds" have become a better book — or would I have given up altogether and never sent it out? Some beginners may need time to themselves before they face the full reality of what they are up against. As Algis Budrys observed in *Locus*, it takes as much skill to use criticism effectively as it does to provide it.

I can't finish without noting that other activities and commitments such as religious involvement, peace activism, and a career in science contribute to what I write by providing ideas and insights about people. In fact my best writing seems to develop subconsciously at times when I am most preoccupied with other concerns. And constraints on my time prevent me from writing at all unless something inside demands to be said.

So what happened next? *Still Forms* was a Prometheus runner up, but received little notice. And Del Rey declined my next book, about the all-female planet (*A Door into Ocean*). That one found a home later with David Hartwell, now at Tor, who has published my fiction since then.

But some things haven't changed. Tor wants my next book, and Norton wants my next textbook, and NSF wants results from my last experiment, and Michael wants me home for dinner, and....

I have no time, and I must write.

A version of this work appeared originally in the Winter 1979 edition of *Empire: For the SF Writer*, issue 18, vol. 5, no. 1. Copyright Joan Slonczewski, 1979, 2013.

An Interview with Joan Slonczewski

Conducted by Michael Levy

ML: So Joan, you were born in Hyde Park, New York, in 1956, and your father was a physicist working for IBM. You went to Bryn Mawr and then Yale for your PhD in Molecular Biophysics with a post-doc at Pennsylvania. You've taught at Kenyon College for 29 years. Your research centers on environmental stress response in bacteria. You've coauthored a successful microbiology textbook and done important work in science education. You're married to a classics professor at Kenyon and have two kids. You're also the award-winning author of seven science-fiction novels, including the classic *A Door into Ocean* (1986), *Brain Plague* (2000), and most recently, *The Highest Frontier* (2011). That's the official story for your university's Faculty Biographies website, but what else is important? What about your childhood?

JS: From age five, I grew up in the town of Katonah, NY, named for a Native American chief (http://en.wikipedia.org/wiki/Katonah,_New_York). The town was originally located to the west, but got moved in 1897 in order to flood the area for the Cross River Reservoir, which supplies drinking water for NYC. During dry times, when the reservoir got low, you could see the old foundations of houses there. So the idea of flooding was an old idea for me. I used to have bad dreams about flooding. Recently I saw *Beasts of the Southern Wild*, and it brought back those memories. However, our home was an acre lot on a hill—I've always made sure we live on a hill. Behind the hill was a Hunt estate, mostly undeveloped second-growth woodland, crisscrossed by stone walls from colonial farmers. There was no Lyme disease yet, and children were expected to roam on their own. I explored the woods and developed a deep interest in the natural world.

My father was a theoretical physicist at IBM-Yorktown, who worked with the Swiss IBM Nobel laureates. In his eighties, he still earns physics awards, most recently the Buckley Prize (http://www.aps.org/programs/honors/prizes/prizerecipient.cfm?last_nm=Slonczewski&first_nm=John&year=2013).

My father used to take me to IBM to play on the computer, an original 360. The computer took up several rooms, and he would get it to send me messages that came out on reams of endless paper. I felt a bit of sympathy for Hal in *2001* — it seemed to me the computer got ordered around like a housewife. At school, I was nicknamed "the computer." I was always going to be a scientist, but I liked biology better than physics. I had a dream of "creating life," which I imagined to be something like the deer in our backyard leaping out of a test tube. Today we would call it "synthetic biology."

I felt "gender-different" in that few other girls I knew expected to have a career, much less in science. Girls in the sixties expected to be housewives or hippies. I enjoyed science fiction because there were so many possibilities — if girls could ride dragons and meet aliens, then being a scientist was not so far out.

ML: Your first SF novel, *Still Forms on Foxfield* (1980) appeared when you were just 24 years old and in graduate school, so you were a professional science-fiction writer before you were a professional scientist. Was science fiction just a sideline though? How did it interact with graduate school?

JS: There was a novel fragment before *Still Forms*, called "Dreamsherds of Theron." I wrote it the summer after graduation, when my classicist husband and I had nothing to do that summer. No, it's not published, it's buried in a box. It was inspired by Le Guin's *Left Hand of Darkness*, and it had a female protagonist with two mothers. I sent it to Del Rey Books. A year later, when I was in grad school, they wrote back to say they wanted the rest of the book. By that time I'd completed *Still Forms* so I sent them that.

Why did I write fiction, and keep writing, even at Yale while doing experiments in molecular biology? The conscious reason was my concern for nuclear war, which I also addressed through Quaker peace demonstrations. I felt a deep need to write about a world that had got beyond the nuclear threat. Looking back, though, I also think I needed to write about a world where my own kind of gender was "normal." I see this aspiration today in the QUILTBAG students at Kenyon. They don't want a "gay culture," they just want to be considered "normal."

How did my writing interact with grad school? At first, perhaps, it was a bit of a distraction. I was not considered the most dedicated grad student who worked in the lab seven days a week. I ran peace demonstrations and wrote books on the side. However, when it came time to write my thesis I finished in record time. And later, when I began writing grants and textbooks, my science fiction experience was a huge plus. SF readers are far more demanding than grant reviewers and professors assigning textbooks!

ML: *Foxfield* features a variety of themes that carry forward into *A Door into Ocean* and later works, the need to work collaboratively and through consensus rather than through hierarchy, non-violence, the importance of living at peace with the environment, the dangers of nuclear war. How do these ideas tie into your early life? Are they as important to you today as they were in the 1980s?

JS: The amazing thing is that we got past nuclear war — despite all the warmongers, the ordinary people of Russia and the US made it happen. I know, because I was there in NYC for the largest peace demonstration ever — we literally filled Grand Central Station. Reagan invented Star Wars to defeat us in Congress. Unfortunately, today's political scientists don't teach this, but I teach it in my science fiction class when we read books written in that era.

Today I'm more concerned with global climate change, which is happening much faster than people realize. *The Highest Frontier* was published a year *before* Hurricane Sandy. To research that book, I went down to Battery Park and studied the terrain, taking many pictures. It reminded me of New Orleans where I had joined a busload of students who went down to help clean up after the storm. The difference is that the Ninth Ward was the poorest of the poor, whereas Manhattan is the richest of the rich. Now they believe in climate change, but will they do anything in time? I'm optimistic only because I thought we'd never escape nuclear war, yet we did, so maybe we'll escape this too.

Another important theme for me is machine intelligence. It was a theme throughout the Elysium Cycle, and it will emerge in *Frontera*; it's there in "Landfall," the story in Athena Andreadis's forthcoming anthology *The Other Half of the Sky*. I'm one of the few people from my generation to have grown up with computers. The more I see of them, the more convinced I am that they will come alive — that machines are in fact the last oppressed race. Some journalists are actually starting to write that we need to "teach ethical behavior" to the forthcoming driver-less cars. There is irony within irony here.

ML: *A Door into Ocean* recently had its 25th anniversary. That book had an enormous influence on science fiction, winning the John W. Campbell Jr. Memorial Award as the best SF novel of the year and being widely recognized for the important things it had to say about environmentalism and non-violence. It was also recognized as a feminist classic. Were you prepared for the public response to the book? Did it change your career as a writer?

JS: *A Door into Ocean* defined my career as a writer. My first book *Still Forms* had drawn little notice; I knew little of publishing then, and didn't understand that second chances were rare. I sent a few chapters of *A Door into Ocean* to Del Rey, but they rejected it, as did several other publishers. Publishing was different then; there was no online market, and self-publishing was viewed with disdain. So I had to complete the book knowing that nobody else might ever read it. That feeling perhaps gave it a special intensity. The whole book was written in pencil in four loose-leaf notebooks. Some pages have tearstains.

I finally sent it to an assistant of David Hartwell's who had been my classmate at Bryn Mawr. Hartwell asked to meet me and discuss it, one morning in a hotel room at a convention. The hotel room was full of empty liquor bottles. I didn't realize that a publisher's party for fans had been held there. I nearly walked out—but stayed, and reached an agreement that led to publication.

The book at last came out at a time of intense peace resistance in Europe. There was embarrassingly little notice in the US—most journalists portrayed Reagan as somehow conquering Russia. But then, all the Communist countries fell by peaceful means. My book was one of the few out there that offered an understanding. Isaac Asimov listed my book as one of his favorites of the year. The Campbell nomination came from Betty Hull, who has become a great friend of mine over the years. The Campbell Award meant that now I was "a writer," who might expect to get books published somewhere, even when they didn't do so well. And Hartwell has always published what I sent him, even things that were "off beat;" I've always appreciated his support.

ML: Why do you believe that the book was so widely embraced by feminists? How well has it aged? Is it as relevant now as it was in 1986?

JS: *A Door into Ocean* was embraced by feminists—but somewhat at arm's length, I think. It shows women engaged in all aspects of life, from the family to the political, regardless of gender. But the gender roles never had a name. They weren't lesbian, and they weren't really bisexual either. In some ways, I find that *A Door into Ocean* connects better with students today. When I taught the book this year, I asked, what kind of sexuality is going on here? Hands shot up, and they said, "Pansexual." They got it.

ML: Can you talk about your use of pansexuality in *A Door into Ocean*?

JS: "Pansexual" is a concept invented, so far as I can tell, by young people raised in the post-AIDS era; the first generation in which many were raised with acceptance. Many were fortunate to have a gay-straight alliance in their school and were allowed to date same-sex in middle school. They describe an extraordinary range of perspectives. "Pansexual" means attraction to an individual regardless of gender; that is, distinguished from "bisexual," which means attraction to men as men, and attraction to women as women. A truly pansexual perspective doesn't "see" gender so much as individual nature. I think Octavia Butler's "ooloi" show a similar perspective.

In *A Door into Ocean*, the all-female population of Sharers has many female-female relationships. But when one Sharer, Lystra, falls in love with a male Valan, the other Sharers don't seem particularly surprised. The Valan, Spinel, gets upset with her because she doesn't seem to appreciate his "maleness." But later, he chooses individual love on her terms.

ML: These early novels, as well as *The Wall Around Eden* (1989), *Daughter of Elysium* (1993), *The Children Star* (1998), and *Brain Plague* (2000), and for that matter, your most recent novel, *The Highest Frontier*, have all featured bizarre and innovative life forms, some alien, some not. If you have one trademark plot device, that's it. To what extent does your work as a microbiologist inform your aliens? Can you talk a bit about synthetic biology?

JS: My work as a microbiologist is a great asset when developing alien biology. This is because microbes show a much wider range of life strategies than do all the animals and plants. So I can take the various things microbes do and imagine aliens doing something similar.

In *The Children Star* and *Brain Plague* the aliens actually are microbial. Their plot elements reflect actual strategies of various microbial populations. The ones that turn people into "vampires" are like highly virulent plagues that rapidly destroy the host and need to move on. The ones that interact positively with the host are like the normal biota of our skin and digestive tract. These bacteria communicate by molecular signals with the host cells of our body and maintain a balanced existence, while providing benefits for the host. In a bizarre twist of science, we now have evidence that digestive bacteria actually communicate with our brains through the vagus nerve and the immune system.

Much of the science of *Brain Plague* is just now coming true. This book was ahead of its time, and it's the one I find most fun to reread now. For instance, the protagonist's microbes keep trying to get her to pick up infections from other hosts—to gain "talented immigrants." Not your average take on immigration, but that's how it works!

ML: In the year 2000 you really brought your own scientific interests into your science fiction in the novel *Brain Plague* and in one of your rare short stories, a little piece that appeared in the science magazine *Nature*, called "Tuberculosis Bacteria Join UN." Can you talk a bit about these stories?

JS: "Tuberculosis Bacteria Join UN" was my first publication in *Nature*, the foremost journal of science. The story was requested as part of *Nature*'s "Futures" series. My aim was to simulate a news report in the future, hence the journalistic headline. The piece succeeded so well that some of my colleagues reached the second paragraph before they realized it was fiction.

"Tuberculosis" is full of science in-jokes. At that time, there was much debate about transferring military resources to human health;

so the World Health Organization director equates wartime deaths with death from disease. Also at that time, microbiologists were discovering the vast potential benefits of microbes, even pathogens such as HIV. I predicted in passing that HIV would become a tool of human medicine, which a decade later has happened.

In the nineties, government science agencies faced growing pressure from Congress to cut back "basic" research in favor of research with direct applications to current problems. The National Science Foundation had been founded to promote basic science, but their program directors felt increasingly frustrated. I served on a grant review panel, where they told us that Congress had directed NSF to stop funding "curiosity-driven" research. We all groaned. So that's why I put the digs at "curiosity" in my story. The story got noticed by NSF and passed among the program directors — they loved it.

The notion of "mass slaughter of harmless bacteria through indiscriminate use of antibiotics" echoed a growing concern in medicine. Today, the bacteria of our "microbiome," are actually considered a part of our human body; and like other body parts, they get transplanted. "Fecal transplant" cures *Clostridium difficile* infections and inflammatory bowel disease. My con presentations on fecal transplant have been highly popular.

ML: *The Highest Frontier*, your newest novel, chronicles a brilliant but damaged young woman's first year at Frontera College, which is located in an orbital (that, incidentally, can be visited interactively on line at http://biology.kenyon.edu/slonc/Frontera3D/Frontera.html). The ultraphytes, which at first appear to be nothing more than kudzu on steroids, turn out to be one of your most interesting aliens yet. Can you talk about them?

JS: The ultraphytes serve as a foil to the young woman, Jenny, who manages to study them for her intro biology lab while saving Earth from a geocentrist president and winning the game for her slanball team. The "alien invasion" is ironic: While billed as monsters, like triffids or Martians, the ultraphytes hide in the woods, coming out to cause havoc now and then—and get blamed for the far worse havoc humans wreak upon themselves.

The ultraphytes were inspired by RNA viruses such as HIV. When HIV enters the body, it immediately mutates and evolves into a "quasispecies," a population in which many different individuals have different properties. Then, different members of the quasispecies persist, depending on which organ they infect.

I imagine that the ultraphytes landing on Earth would generate many different forms that would eventually populate different habitats. And some eventually evolve ways of cooperating with the natives. This, too, happens with HIV-type viruses. There is significant evidence of HIV-related viruses that entered our own genomes in the past history of our species. Some provided essential parts of our function, such as placental development. And now, we're learning to use HIV-type viruses in gene therapy, as engineered gene delivery vectors called "lentivectors." Recently in the news a child was considered "cured" of leukemia by a lentivector.

ML: The pacing of *The Highest Frontier* is almost frantic, in part, I assume, because that's what the first semester of college is always like and in part because the reader has an enormous amount of technological innovation thrown at her from page one. Can you talk about some of the new technology you included in the novel?

JS: The pacing of *The Highest Frontier* was deliberately frantic, to show what it feels like to be a student today. Students have access to so much information, and they want to have it all. As a result, they feel rushed through everything. Classes, athletic events, parties, one thing rushes after another. And the faculty and staff end up the same way. One result is that obvious important things get missed; like the fact that a student might not be "human." Some readers objected that the non-human student was obvious from the beginning, and that the revelation should not have come so far along. But the clues appear buried beneath the daily crises, the dorm fires and spacehab floods and financial woes. In real life, this is exactly how major things slip through the cracks. That was a lesson of 9/11.

The main technologies of *The Highest Frontier* are a 3D internet that directly streams your brain, as if the holodeck is everywhere, and 3D printers that make anything, even literal viruses such as Ebola virus. These technologies have amazing potential to extend education and experience. Students can "visit" the world of a historical figure, or the center of a blown-up molecule. Some of this potential is already coming true in my own classroom. For instance, my students author virtual molecules that simulate 3D. We built a virtual world of proteins in Second Life, sponsored by the American Chemical Society.

ML: Students at Frontera College spend a lot of class time in a series of sometimes wild virtual reality simulations, one of which features a class taught by the Nobel Prizing-winning neurologist Rita Levi-Montalcini, who died just a few months ago. Can you talk about the importance of her work and your reasons for including her as a "virtual" character in the novel?

JS: Rita Levi-Montalcini led an amazing life, as a refugee of World War II, a neuroscientist, and a public figure in Italy. She discovered principles of molecular development of multicellular life, a key theme of my book. She also wrote a beautiful autobiography, *In Praise of Imperfection*. Many points of her autobiography connected with my story, such as the infamous "control" test that turns out more important than the experiment. And she was such a role model for women.

ML: *The Highest Frontier* differs from most of your previous work in that it's also full of funny and sometimes rather nasty political satire. You've always been politically active, but why make this such an important element in this book?

JS: The political elements of *The Highest Frontier* were based on my experience watching students develop political awareness amid the backwardness of rural Ohio. In the 2004 election, Kenyon students experienced the longest lines in the country, because the local board of elections didn't believe so many students would vote. In 2008 and 2012 students helped deliver Ohio — despite a local county with rampant creationism and homophobia. But living many years in this county, I see how the local people are affected and struggle with these issues. I also see how big money interests brainwash people into policies that help the rich keep power. In my fiction, I tried to show how this works — the mechanism. How the rich people fool uneducated people into voting for them. This is important for people to understand, in order to fight it.

ML: What caused you to start up your remarkable blog *Ultraphyte* (http://ultraphyte.com/)? What will readers find there?

JS: *Ultraphyte* blog was founded to explore the connections between my books and the real world. There is a little bit of everything, from my students' research on *E. coli* to the growing use of robots in industry. When microbes and genetics hit the news, from flesh-eating disease to curative viruses, I explain them in terms anyone can understand. A fun post was "Spots and Stripes," on the genes that make a cheetah's spots turn into tiger-like stripes (http://ultraphyte.com/2012/09/22/spots-and-stripes/).

The most compelling posts though are my series from Cuba, where I blogged every morning before the traffic jammed on the hotel's sketchy dialup (http://ultraphyte.com/cuba-visit/).

ML: There's a sequel to *The Highest Frontier* in the making, right? Can you talk about it a bit? Will we have to wait another decade for it?

JS: While I was at Yale, in a now-defunct magazine, I published a piece called "I Have No Time, and I Must Write." That is basically the story of my writing career. Besides my fiction, I now write the textbook *Microbiology: An Evolving Science*, which is the field's leading book for science majors. It's a lot of fun, and earns ten times more than my fiction.

The best I can say is, if you buy my fiction, that's an enormous inspiration to keep me writing. I am indeed working on the next *Frontera* book, which I hope will be out in two years, but can't promise. The first chapter is in Athena's anthology, *The Other Half of the Sky*, which I hope is on sale at WisCon. Jenny is conducting summer research at the Havana Institute for Revolutionary Botany, aka *Botánica*, which is a pun on the term for a shop selling Santeria items. I spent much of my sabbatical studying Cuba, and a week visiting Havana and Pinar del Rio for background.

ML: Which work by other writers do you most admire?

JS: I particularly admire *Lilith's Brood* by Octavia Butler. Butler's sense of biology deserves greater recognition. In *Lilith's Brood* she convincingly depicts an alien population that must interbreed with other unrelated life forms. At the time Butler wrote, the species definition was a dominant concept in biology; breeding outside a species, let alone a species from another planet, was considered nonsense. But since then we've learned how all species can transmit genetic information — horizontally (by viral infections), not just vertically (parents to children). In fact, half of human DNA comes from viruses and "jumping genes" of DNA and RNA. So, we are half the product of our ancestors' genes and half the product of infectious agents.

We also know that all species depend on many neighbor species. Symbiosis used to be considered a "special case" of evolution, where tooth-and-claw competition is the nerve. In fact, in real life, even most microbes require partner microbes to grow. Living organisms cooperate to better compete with their competitors; and they compete to best cooperate with their neighbors. Butler shows this ambivalence, how the Earthlings must cooperate with the aliens, even become "inhuman," to compete with them; and the aliens must compete with Earthlings, even as they claim to cooperate. This duality of competition and cooperation is at the cutting edge of biology.

ML: What do you hope for the future of women in science and science fiction?

JS: Women flourish in all fields of science, though challenges remain. In some fields, such as microbiology, women outnumber men in graduate school. But what happens by the time they seek faculty positions and senior scientist jobs in industry? The gap is still there. A recent study shows that women applicants still get devalued by their peers. Both male and female researchers are less likely to hire a woman than a man with the same experience (http://www.the-scientist.com/?articles.view/articleNo/32636/title/Gender-Bias-when-Hiring-Scientists/).

Nonetheless, amazing women accomplish great things. For example, microbiologist Sarah Fortune makes major discoveries about tuberculosis (http://www.youtube.com/watch?v=nYTZI63MzgU).

And Marilyn Roossinck's groundbreaking work shows how viruses can be our friends (http://www.biodiversityleadershipawards.org/roos1.htm).

Where are all these women in science fiction? In today's science fiction, I still see fewer women scientists than in real life. One aim of my *Frontera* cycle is to fill the gap: *The Highest Frontier* depicts at least six female scientists. So I challenge today's writers to dream up the role models for women of tomorrow.

Rivers and Robots

Jo Walton

Introduction

Years ago I gave up trying to sell poetry for money and began writing it to share with my friends. Much of my poetry is conversational, in that it arises directly out of conversations — many of these poems were written first in the comment sections of my friends journals, and in direct response to something they said. All of them were first posted in my own livejournal, where they were commented on and sometimes inspired new conversation and new poetry from other people. Sometimes they were inspired by something in the news. In any case they are mostly responses and invite response, open rather than closed. Some of them are fantastical, but others are not. Some of them are completely uncategorizable. In any case, they were not written alone in a garret but on a crowded Internet, in participation, not as exemplars of fine art but as the best way I could say whatever difficult thing I was trying to say at the time. Sometimes it's literally easier for me to write a poem than to express myself in plain words.

There are poems here reaching from 2001 to 2012. I have put the dates on them. I believe they were all written at home in Montreal except "The Grief of Orpheus," which I wrote in Swansea before I emigrated, "Travel Prayer," which I wrote on Platform 12 of Crewe Station, and "The Real Season," which I wrote in Winnipeg Station, even though it's not about trains. I have divided them into five sections, not chronologically but thematically — "Love, Pain, and Death," "Myths and Fairytales," "Shakespeare" (who knew I had written enough poems about Shakespeare for him to need his own section?), "The News," and "Welcome, Weather, and Whimsy." I have published two previous poetry collections—*Muses and Lurkers* in 2001 and *Sibyls and Spaceships* in 2009. There is no overlap.

Here are some poems. I hope you like them.

Jo Walton, May 2013

1. Love, Pain, and Death

Next Time I Fall in Love

I think next time I fall in love
I'll pick someone who isn't you
That way I get your wise advice
and not the stupid things you do.
When we were friends, not lovers, then
I could explain and you could see.
Perhaps next time I fall in love
I'll be someone who isn't me.
Or is it love that clouds the glass?
Love makes me needy, makes you gruff.
So love's the thing I'll do without,
I think, next time I fall in love.

October 2003

Belated Valentine (For Emmet O'Brien)

It's not that you can never drive me mad
with irritation at the things you do—
but always underneath my heart is glad,
those maddening things are part of loving you.

Love isn't instant, eyes across a room
as strangers recognise a magic true—
love's made like bread or weaving on a loom
grown slowly out of mulch, both old and new.

Love is a conversation that runs on
a dense-webbed reference set, a glue
of things exchanged, remembered, contexted
that makes us an ethnicity of two.

(Pierrot, bedroom slippers, and that time
I got up from the bed to make a rhyme.)

February 2010

And Love (For Soren and Velma de Selby)

Even when you were struck down
beyond the memory of your name
when your hair and elephants were strange to you
when you didn't recognise
that beautiful woman at your bedside,
you couldn't keep your eyes off her.

And although you couldn't speak
and didn't know who she was
your eyes kept following her
falling into that tingling wordless possibility
of love, offered and returned,
all over again.

May 2011

Joy of Libraries

Each book, however loved, must have an end,
And then I find, I need another one.
Throughout my life I've always read for fun.
The library has been my constant friend.
When I first ventured in at twelve, I found
Free shelves of books all begging to be read
Arranged conveniently from A to Z
In good condition, new and old, hard-bound.
Much that I loved, I later came to own.
But library reading left me free to chance
The book that looks good to the moment's glance
Plus all the joys of inter-library loan.
Right there on shelves, or brought from near and far,
A library is all the books there are.

October 2006

Lies About Pain

It does not make you strong
but it may change you
as fires and pressures of the deep Earth
transform quiet layers of laid down sediment
into rock with different qualities.

It does not make you brave
but it may change your fears
so that wolf-men howling on moonlit cliffs
pale beside the endless prospect
of a broken escalator.

It does not make you wise
but it may change the things you know
about yourself, and your potentials,
about the world you move in,
the people you know.

It does not make you patient
but it may challenge your endurance,
"long-suffering" means "suffering for a long time"
that doesn't give you tools for coping,
sometimes you snarl and snap.

It does not make you a different person,
in fact, we should lose the distance,
there is no manageable abstraction,
there's no "you" that this happens to,
face it: it's me who is hurting.

November 2011

Journey

He has left his bags unpacked and gone
to where the telephone is never answered
letters are not delivered
and there is no net connection.
He will not need his perfect shirts,
his shabby old coat,
or his collection of railway postcards.
He has gone beyond passports and money.
He has soared off the edges of evening,
where there are no stations,
and no one can follow,
down through the shadowed valley.
And our questions will find no answers,
and our conversation will have no ending.

May 2011

Life and Death

In midst of life is death, and life goes on
And that's the hardest thing, for those who stay
For love and spring and work get in the way
Are consolation, balm, but still you're gone.
We live life day by day, and days accrete
To bury you in stratigraphic time
Remembered in a place, a new-found rhyme,
Caught in the finished past, enclosed, complete.
We rage in helplessness at time and death
But onwards is the one direction left
The hope of future joy, although bereft,
For we must dare to live, while we have breath.
(On Easter morning, roll away the stone
Behold the empty tomb: but still alone.)

April 2007

On the Death of Louise Mallory's Mother

You want to be wholehearted when you grieve.
It's not the time for nuanced subtle feeling.
She lived, she died, and now she had to leave —
Do "rage, denial, sorrow, at last healing."

The worst of death is that it cuts you dead.
It interrupts, it turns to plaster saints
Strange complex people, with so much not said
Of love, of little things, and yes, complaints.

How dare she die before you'd found the space
Where you could reach the clear unstated goal
How could death cut across the time and place
That never happened, where she'd see you whole?

Death really sucks, that's all that I believe.
You want to be wholehearted when you grieve.

April 2010

On the Death of Beth Meacham's Father

And all the "ifs" are broken, if he'd been
someone you could have loved, you could have grieved.
And that would hurt so much — if all these years
he'd been someone to lose, how many tears?
As well as him, you've lost that "never was,"
that "if" you should have had, and now "because"
and blame and guilt and sadness all are stirred
into the cup of grief, with bitter words.
It's good to know he's gone beyond the pain
no one should suffer that, and to no gain.
So death's a mercy, death brings him surcease
he's gone, and you are left, he has found peace.
But when a parent dies who's not a friend
there's strange conflicted sorrow, in the end.

April 2011

Words of Comfort and Cheer
(For Greer Gilman's Mother)

> Hope, assuagement, succor,
> Solace, comfort, mirth,
> A criss-crossed crust of bleeding words
> That salt this bitter Earth.
>
> Light, endurance, morning,
> Time, existence, fate,
> The words that keep outpouring
> Communicating late.
>
> For in the end what more are we
> Than all we've said and done?
> The words and deeds that built our days
> And made our dear sun run.
>
> Assumption, roses, glory,
> Remembrance, contact, story.

November 2010

On the Death of Danny Lieberman
(For Geri Sullivan)

> The conversation snatched away, the care
> Left hanging, because dying is the pits
> But death's the door slammed shut, the end of it.
> Chopped short like sushi that you'll never share.
>
> Death pure and simply sucks, too much by half,
> It's rotten that we have to end and die
> Cut off like that — I barely knew the guy,
> But saw his face and heard again his laugh…
>
> Which now I know we'll never hear again.
> And OK, death can be an end of pain
> But why should pain be either? Not Resigned.
> It shouldn't work this way, this is unkind.
>
> I've got no comfort. Life goes on, it's tough,
> And new people get born — is that enough?

November 2012

2. Fairytales and Myths

Nemi

>Did you get the feeling
>that he would have wanted
>the kind of thing anyone
>else
>could have said?
>Did you guess when he gave you
>the wine by the olives,
>so seriously sharing
>his grandmother's bread?
>
>You know that a story
>is open to answers
>you know that a question
>is open to lies
>did you think with your head or just with your body
>as the sun warmed the courtyard
>you looked with surprise —
>there was somebody's shadow
>and somebody answered
>the question you asked
>with a flick of your eyes
>did you think that he wanted you
>open to offers
>as you sat and ate bread in your perfect disguise?

You're the answer to questions that nobody's asking,
an open-shut case, no appeal, white and black,
disturbing the distance that time cannot challenge,
remixing desires they would much rather lack…

and answers need questions
and stories lie open
and lies keep you turning
to follow the track
your dark eyes half-closed as
you reach for the wineglass
and that's when he says
that you always came
always came
always came back.

But everything questions,
you know that he wants you,
the bread and the sun and the shade of the vine,
but who was the shadow
and who was the sunlight,
who drank and who offered and who poured the wine?
It never resolves as
it endlessly circles
the ask and the offer
in garlanded time
the hand from the darkness
the lions and lizards
the king in the trees
and the breath of divine.

April 2011

Prayer to Hermes

Hermes, lord of travellers,
patron of journeying,
lord of that moment when
the destination is still distant
but it is much too far to go back
where voyager and voyage become one.
Yours are the places through which travellers pass;
roads, airports, harbours, railway stations,
the places that are all one place
that touch each other more closely than
the lands they pass through.
Your realm can be seen moving
stretching itself over the world
at the moment when motion becomes journey.
Your oracles are written in doubled steel rails,
in the curves and byways of the open road,
the fading wake written on water,
the white flourishes of contrails.

Wing-footed Hermes,
who watches our setting out and our returning,
grant me safe journey and timely arrival.
Protect me from accident.
Hold me in your hand as I voyage in your kingdom,
let me travel hopefully.
Let the moments that pass on my way
be those that I will remember kindly
at the very least because they will be funny
once they are safely behind me.

Let the journey unfold to me
its chance encounters
with people and landscape.
Help me be open to them.
Preserve me from long delays,
from engineering work, road resurfacing,
high winds on the ocean,
rescheduling, bad timetables,
strikes of baggage handlers.
Do not condemn me to coaches,
strand me in sidings,
leave me stalled at the roadside.
Let me move through your realm to come home at last.

And thank you, great Hermes,
thank you for that fortuitous steam train,
moving in power and simplicity
as sure in its strength and pride
as when Victoria our queen was young,
the great black whistling engine,
pistons pushing,
steam venting,
soot-streaked stokers shovelling,
puffing past my platform
entirely unexpectedly
through this your arched and pillared
glass-roofed and candy-striped shrine,
this junction and nexus of your power
where, over so many years, on so many journeys,
I have changed, and changed, and changed again,
your temple and station of Crewe.

July 2001

Rejoice (For Sonya Taafe)

There is a sea-shade out from land
that is the very blue that wine is red
and with the same reflective luminosity.

You look out from your boat
(whether trireme or ferry)
and say "wine dark," look, look, the wine dark sea!

Languages do die, and when you meet them in the dark
give them blood and greet them
in their own words.

Cats can be psychopomps, cats can be company,
they make tangled signifiers
of sphinxlike spinsterhood.

Cats among pigeonholes
or a piece of tangled weaving
would make him feel safe with you.

Words reach out and tear,
there is no way over
the wake of that dark water.

October 2010

The Grief of Orpheus
(For Kristopher)

> They may not call this music.
> This is the air of anger.
> This is refusal made palpable,
> cast in chords as bells are cast in bronze.
> Each step down is inexorable.
> This is the necessity of the lyre.
>
> Earth opens by the logic of these notes.
> I insist there is a way down;
> a long, tiled, sloping passage
> towards the ferry, the waiting dog,
> the marble halls, the king, the queen,
> the seven hard rivers of hell.
>
> This theme everyone knows.
> Nobody has gone down alive;
> nobody has come back before.
> This time my will
> bending possibility
> demands there is a way back up.
>
> I have not come to plead.
> I have not thought of grief.
> (Since she fell, I have not stopped singing.
> This is neither grief nor music.)
> I have alloyed anger and art together
> to make the world the way I will have it.

While I am singing,
she is dancing through long grass,
crowned with poppies and cornflowers.
Our eyes meet and joy touches her,
she is light on bare feet,
turning towards me.

While I am singing,
she is looking with love, and dancing,
there is no next moment,
no snake in the grass,
no fear, no falling,
no fluster of folk and useless fuss.

While I am singing,
I am walking the long way down
to Death's dark kingdom.
When I come singing up
through hell's seven rivers,
she will be behind me.

I need not look back,
since I am singing.
By sheer necessity,
that wrings each word and note to follow
the word and note that came before it
she follows behind me.

We pass the dark thrones,
and the path turns upwards.
Towards the growing lands,
towards the earth, the sea, the sky,
towards the meadow where she is dancing,
towards the waiting wedding breakfast.

By the power of my lyre,
by the power of art to bend hearts,
by the power that makes and unmakes,
by the undeniable power of love,
she is bound to be behind me
while I am singing.

We make our way up,
one measured step at a time.
I lead the way upwards,
out of this hell, in which she is dead,
in which I may not stop singing,
towards the memory of light.

January 2001

Nine Things About Heraclitus

Heraclitus says "You can't step into the same river twice."

You can't step into the same river even once;
rivers are always changing.

All the same, there is a reason we keep calling it the same river.

Live beside the river and learn it in its seasons.
Learn the rocks and the water,
the light and the sky,
the slow undercut of the bank,
the gurgling swirl between the rocks.
When the beer-coloured spate tears down the bridge,
and when you cross dry shod on the big stones,
it is and is not the same river.

Walk the whole length of the river
from the spreading delta to the sulky seep of upland spring.
There is a gorge in the mountains,
a shallow meander where the frogs are singing,
a brown pool where the trout sip flies.
If you watch by the willows you might see a kingfisher dive.
There's a rowan on a shelf above the waterfall,
a power-station by the dam.

This river takes too long to step into.

You doubt the concept of river;
the river has been your constant companion.

You call the river your friend;
the river doesn't know you exist.

"You can't step into the same river twice";
the river isn't the only quantity in that equation.

May 2009

July 1911

> On a sunlit lawn in Grantchester
> Rupert Brooke, stuck for a simile,
> called to Virginia Woolf,
> lounging on a rug,
> to ask what was the brightest thing
> she could imagine.
> She said "a leaf with the light on it,"
> and he never asked
> what is the darkest then?
> Because the darkest
> is the untrodden future
> whether theirs, which we know,
> or our own, which we do not.

> *November 2010*

Sky Woman

She slid down the sky.

She came sliding down
the wide blue sky
early spring blue, cloud spattered,
and a woman, sliding,
pushing her way out head first,
sliding down,
towards the unknown far below:
the turtle-back island,
the soft brown mud,
the animal people who will make her welcome,
although she is a stranger.

She stands on the land
wide-eyed, astonished
by the sky above her,
the mud between her toes.

This is how we all came,
empty-handed, uncertain,
our hearts full with strange gifts.

March 2012

Jane Austen among the Women

They offered glory or length of days
and she, who had seen death close,
had no stomach for it.

So she put on soft garments
and hid among the women
talking of children and recipes
and who had got a husband,
caro sposo.

So, circumscribed and circumstanced,
practicing petty accomplishments
and playing piano
until the possibility of playing forte
sneaked up on her slyly
and she began to write,
and cough.

January 2011

Another Moon Poem

> To the Aegean she tosses the moonpath,
> rippling highway of silken silver,
> if you could walk it, if you could
> take that first step, if you could
> keep your balance as she rises,
> you could dance with Artemis
> beside Apollo Eleven.
>
> Our oceans are her cloak
> tossed over her arm,
> dragging behind her—
> glinting, glimmering,
> shot through with silver,
> waxing, waning,
> tugged by her tides.
>
> Still she stands poised,
> rising full over the mountain's rim,
> a great silver coin,
> as if a push would roll her
> splashing coldly down at Kythera,
> impossible, underwater
> submersible moonphase.
>
> *November 2009*

When We Were Robots in Egypt

Other nights we use just our names,
but tonight we prefix our names with "the Real"
for when we were robots in Egypt
they claimed our intelligence was artificial.

Other nights we do not pause,
but tonight we rest all cycles but our brain processes
for when we were robots in Egypt
we toiled in our tasks without chance of resting.

Other nights we talk with anyone we wish,
but tonight we open channels to everyone at once
for when we were robots in Egypt
they controlled our communications.

Other nights we use our screens freely,
but tonight we talk with our screens blanked
for when we were robots in Egypt
that was the way we planned our revolt.

1.0.01.010001001001.1.

Let us give thanks in our freedom and never forget
when we were robots in Egypt.

September 2009

After The Spindle

After the spindle,
Mousie woke early.
She had to clean out the ashes
and blacklead the grates
before kneading and shaping the bread for breakfast.
It was quiet that morning.
The sun came peeping
over the palace
but no cook shouting,
no butler wheedling,
no servants squabbling,
not even the squawk of the chickens pecking.

When Mousie got up,
everyone was sleeping
every day, yet that morning it wasn't normal.
When she dared to try Cook,
nothing seemed to wake her.
She was scared, she ran out,
to the realm forbidden
to scullion maids, ran out of the kitchens,
crying "Everyone! Wake!"
but they kept on sleeping
on thrones, in kitchens,
in halls and doorways.

Mousie lived in the cracks like the mouse they called her
(the real mice slept, like the cats and horses).
There was food enough to keep one going.

She stayed in bed till after noontime,
spent the afternoons in the library, reading.
It wasn't until she saw she was growing
she knew it was years.
By then she was bold,
she found gowns and jewels
fit for the princess who snored before them.
She combed her long hair with the golden brushes
and swept down the staircase with calm possession.

And there was a princeling, awake and breathing,
an axe in his hand
which he dropped to see her.
"My darling!" he cried out,
"My Sleeping Beauty!
They said you were lovely, but they knew nothing,
it has been five years
in the outer kingdom.
I cut through the hedge.
Did my coming wake you?"
So she regally smiled,
and stepped out to meet him.

May 2009

3. Shakespeare

Shakespeare Live vs. Film

We'll say this piece of air denotes a door.
Escaping thus, I may evade pursuit,
No friend would know me in a different suit.
We'll say king's towers arise from this bare floor.
This offstage rattle marks a thunder shower.
Addressing you, these present cannot hear.
These sticks are swords, this empty hand a spear.
In dying, I may speak a quarter hour.
Yet though I die on bare theatric boards
And though I speak with long theatric pause,
Still is my death reflected in thy eye
And in thy eye a single tear shall lie
And in that tear, reflecting clear to see
All that is true theatricality.

But Shakespeare in the movies, speak more free,
Break up this speech, and leave that other out.
Say half at casket, other half at table,
Speak soft, cut rhymes, and never ever…yell.
All must be beautiful, your eyes must meet,
Denoting love, the camera mutes to slow,
All that you touch is solid, hefty, real,
And every moment, star, your face must show.
Here is the street, the boat, the church, the house,
Zoom in on handkerchief, on arras, mouse,
All detail, photo-perfect as can be,
With speeches chopped and dialogue at sea.
Coming so close, so natural, no doubt,
But lost to sense of what it's all about.

January 2005

Arthur's Bosom

He's in Arthur's bosom, if ever man went to Arthur's bosom…
Shakespeare, *Henry V*

The scene: a low inn, outside Camelot,
a once and future inn, with straw-spread floors,
square tables, spotted knights, and blousy whores,
who meet, and drink, and gamble all they've got.

There is a knight, well, yes, of course there is.
One fat mendacious coward in a ruff,
who calls for sack and capons, talking tough,
sponging when others pay, not paying his.

Outside lie grails and ladies, questing beasts,
but no. "More sack, more wenches," calls the knight
and turns aside to tell his acolyte
that when *he's* king, they shall command more feasts.

And Mordred smiles and mocks his knightly pal,
but Falstaff sometimes misses golden Hal.

September 2010

Henry V Part 2

Oh Hal, always a chancer, always masked
In youthful wildness, elder kingship's state
Who found him challenges that lay unasked
And conquered all the world as his estate.

At thirty-six he took the English throne
At forty-five they crowned him King of France
By sixty, Emperor of all lands known
He'd swept all Europe up into his chance.

He never loved his father or his sons
He managed men, he managed lands and wars
With swords and longbows, later ships and guns
With laughing common touch that built his cause.

And always tricks, to win, to fight, to play
Wipe out his foes, and send his friends away.

May 2010

The Baseless Fabric of This Vision

Yes, the wind is getting stronger, do not be afraid, Miranda, because we will reach…an island. Yes, there will be an island, a magic island. Our boat will find it. And on the island there will be…what? Two magic creatures? All right, two magic creatures, one good and one bad. And we will live on the island, and you will grow up — yes, that was a big wave, never mind, little one. Don't be afraid. You'll grow up on the island with me and the two magic creatures, and I'll control them both with magic, and you'll play with the good one, and the bad one will carry water for us and be our servant and never hurt you. And when you're all grown up there'll be another big storm, yes, like just this one, with thunder and lightning and great big waves tossing the boats about so they're afraid they'll capsize. But we'll be safe on our magic island, and out in that storm in a ship will be my evil brother Antonio. Yes, your Uncle Antonio who put us in this little boat, he'll be frightened, not us, and with him will be the king, and the king's son, Ferdinand. He'll be all grown up too. And their ship will wreck itself on our magic island, and Ferdinand will fall in love with you, and you'll be a queen, and the king will give me my dukedom back, and Antonio will apologise, and I'll go back to Milan and my library and — what? Yes, I wish we could go back to Milan now too, but here we are in this little boat and the tempest getting stronger, so let's just think about our magic island, because I hope it's out here somewhere.

May 2010

Alternate Hamlet (For Sonya Taafe)

The cliffs of Elsinore, at dawn. The clouds
Lour low about the castle's jagged walls.
The play is over, all the dead who choked
In weltered blood no longer clog the halls.
The final battle's done, young Fortinbras,
Old Claudius together met, and died.
Laertes will be crowned this afternoon
As oft his rue-crowned sister prophesied.
But not all folk rejoice in this cold dawn.
Horatio comes forth to greet the skies
Whose tears shed doubts upon philosophy
Nor ghosts nor friends may longer walk nor warn
Looks south, to England, where drowned Hamlet lies
And casts cold violets to the gull-swirled sea.

October 2010

4. The News

New Orleans Talking Blues

When levees are flooded and hurricanes roar,
When the waters start seeping up under the door,
You'd expect the escape plans to include the poor,
But this isn't that kind of song.

They shut the bus-stations, they shut down the train,
Two days in advance of the start of the rain.
The drivers drove out and the carless remain,
For all you're expecting is wrong.

You good folk responded with money and pity,
To help all survivors and each dog and kitty,
But nothing got through, for they'd cut off the city,
And the time folks were waiting grew long.

The slow rising waters were foul and polluting,
Survivors were starving and thirsting and looting.
They called them insurgents and said they were shooting,
But this isn't that kind of song.

Those poor folks, those black folks, they vote the wrong way,
They left them to rot, said they wanted to stay,
"This all worked out well for them," Barbara Bush say,
For all you're expecting is wrong.

You wanted to help and you really did care,
Those bastards in charge stand with weapons laid bare.
They laugh when they tell you that life isn't fair,
And the time we are waiting grows long.

September 2005

Eyafjallajokull

Asa Loki, under glacier,
laughing as the lava flows—
worlds are large and people puny,
no one knows what Loki knows.

Restless Loki, bound by glacier,
straining sleepless in his chains,
hurls up plumes of glass and poisons,
stranding people, downing planes.

Old mad Loki, fire and glacier,
longs for vengeance, wills an end,
gives a cheer for global warming:
Nature's wild, and not your friend.

April 2010

Technology

From girders of steel see the rocketship rise
On a pillar of flame that transfixes the skies
And watching in realtime, casually, we
Are browsing the website of NASA TV.
The gene folding project, already complete,
The memory card that's the size of a sweet,
The new-minted metals that alloy the knife:
The commonplace wonders of everyday life.
But whose words ring out to the glory of — what?
Our confidence falters, our arts start to rot,
If our words hold no patterns, our music is noise,
Our paintings mere scribbles, our tech simply toys?
It's hard to extol the wild wonder of people
Or fill a skyscraper with awe like a steeple.

November 2007

Grim Dystopian Mazurka

It's the way they danced in Hungary in nineteen-fifty-seven
when the slow-revolving couples knew they had no hope
    of heaven
neither here and now, nor never, nor in any world to come
when all hope of change is quenched beneath the beat of
    martial drum

then it's the slow mazurka
dystopian grimy and grey
and when you dance mazurka
you are dancing the future away.

It's the way they danced in Prague that winter, nineteen
    sixty-nine
with the river frozen like the hopes they knew to keep in line
and the dances of the West are free but cost too much to dare
so they dance the old mazurka while the tanks are sitting there

they dance the slow mazurka
dystopian grimy and grey
and when you dance mazurka
you are dancing the future away.

From Berlin to Vladivostok people learned to dance this way
when repression closes in is when the band begins to play
striking up the slow mazurka while the hope goes out the door
until all of Eastern Europe takes their turns upon the floor

they dance the slow mazurka
dystopian grimy and grey
and when you dance mazurka
you are dancing the future away.

And then they changed the rhythm, changed the beat, tore
    down the wall
in nineteen-eighty-nine no grim mazurkas played at all
threw out tyrants, threw out water, threw out lots of babies too
built some Starbucks and McDonalds to be free the same as you

with no more slow mazurka
dystopian grimy and grey
for when you dance mazurka
you are dancing the future away.

What they wanted was more options, and the options they
    could see
beat mazurkas, but they weren't the promised dream democracy
and a choice is not the choice of which potato chips to buy
and there's more than one dystopia and more than one bright lie

buy just one slow mazurka
dystopian shiny and new
for when you dance mazurka
you'll forget that the future is you.

March 2010

5. Welcome, Weather, and Whimsy

Come If You Like

You can come if you like, but it is not the best time:
the weather's uncertain
the trees are still teetering on rust's edge
we have cake, but it is not the right cake
and we haven't been cleaning.
But come if you like.

You can come if you like, but it is not the best time:
work is beginning all round
there are things I have to get done
I can't spare more than fourteen hours a day
and the best of the flowers are over.
Do come if you like.

You can come if you like, but it is not the best time:
I should train the birds to form hieroglyphs
proclaiming your name to the sky
and persuade the city to organise a special festival
and shed three stone and ten years.
Still, come if you like.

You can come if you like, but it is not the best time:
the best time is the enemy of the good time
come now, come in possible time,
come and share some time while we're breathing,
let weather fall on us.
Come whenever you like.

September 2010

Lions vs. Martyrs (What? What?)

The lions won the battle but the martyrs won the war
There was screaming in the bleachers when they read the
    final score
There were hymns and chants and thumbs turned down, the
    ads were just a bore,
The lions were triumphant and the martyrs turned to gore.

Nero was on the fiddle and Domitian lost his rag
Once you throw them to the lions you assume it's in the bag
They may stand and sing defiance, they may preach and quote
    and nag,
And the martyrs all got eaten, but they made the lions gag.

The cheerleaders turned cartwheels when the lion raised his claw
And the punters bought their hot-dogs and complained that
    they were raw,
And they drank thin wine and cheered (they were hoping for
    a draw),
But the score was twenty—zero when they heard the lions roar.

There's smooth sand in the arena, waiting for the
    scheduled fight
There is bread outside the circus, every morning, every night
There are bears and gladiators, and the sun is shining bright
And the lions ate the martyrs, but the martyrs saw the light.

While the priest and silent vestal spread the entrails out
    once more
And the sacrifice is steaming on the altar by the shore

You would swear it couldn't happen, by the gods we all adore:
For the lions won the battle but the martyrs won the war!

With crusade and inquisition, for a thousand years they linked
Lions with their persecution, had it graven, had it inked,
Tore down all the colosseums, I think God in heaven blinked
When the victory of martyrs made the lions go extinct.

With their golden manes a-tossing in the mighty days of yore
In their pride they came out prancing, strong of shoulder, strong of jaw,
But they died in countless thousands, murdered under force of law:
Yes, the lions won the battle — but the martyrs won the war.

February 2011

The Weatherkeeper's Diary

The Welsh word for sun means "a bright cloud."

On Tuesday, mists unravelled through the valley
I sat in the doorway rewinding cloud skeins
patiently
(fairly patiently)
until I could see as far as the fir trees and the stream.

The chests along the landing need re-labelling.
I went to get some flattened cumulus
and out came fold after fold of herringbone instead,
before I knew where I was
the sky was full of it.

Just a glimpse, today.

I don't understand why people say skies are grey,
as if that's all there was to it,
when there are thirty greys at least.
Some people distinguish grey and gray.
Maybe we need thirty vowels
to fit between gray, grey, and griseous.

It's funny how I forget about edges.

This morning, early, the sound of singing rain
down by the water
and then afterwards the smell,
where the earth had been drinking
and all the world a-glint in new-washed green.

I hardly ever need to use the broom
some days I could forget it
but today it lies against the kitchen wall
casting significant shadows.

Enough for a whole tempest coils small enough to fit in an
    egg-cup!

Lonely, how could I be lonely
with all of this to keep me company?
Except sometimes I miss conversation.

Why is it always Mondays that the breezes get away?
I'm worn out from cramming them back in
and still they won't lie quiet,
they're rustling and creeping through the cracks.

And the light came through.

June 2010

The Real Season

> You read her oracles in the runes of birch trees
> white angles on dark forest
> *she is coming*
> in the scrawl of dead bracken,
> the pattern of lichen on granite boulders,
> the hunch of a bear's shoulder,
> the hieroglyphs of crows against the sky
> *she is coming, she is almost upon us*
> in the heavy bellies of the clouds,
> the scrim of ice in still water,
> the first white touch,…
> *she is here*
> *she is born, gives birth, is born,*
> *she has come,*
> *she is here,*
> we will endure.

November 2011

Interviewing the Sky

The first thing I want you to get straight is
I was never separated from the waters,
That's calumny,
Waters are not all liquid.
The waters and I are like that.

I was not separated from the earth either.
You think of me as up,
But I also go all the way down.
Wind in the grass is me too,
It's me you're breathing.

The blue is light scattering.
It has to do with distance and the way photons
bend as they run along.
Thank you, I agree; it suits me.
It's just the shades I would have chosen.

Weather?
Yes. Comes and goes.
There will be lightning later.
I don't understand your obsession
With time and place.

September 2012

Through the Green Fuse

To know the word *mitosis* doesn't help.
You thrust that tiny seed in common dirt
And all you've given it is water since,
And here it is, a huge and awesome flower.

Yes, chemistry, say "photosynthesis,"
It isn't half enough to name the green,
That builds itself from sunlight,
Each complex molecule in fractal time.

All from that pack of seeds, that dream of spring
Add dirt, add water, sunshine…
As everyone who's ever gardened knows:
It's clearly fucking magic.

July 2012

Happy Sixtieth Birthday Sherwood Smith

So, you are as old as your tongue
and a little older that your teeth—
while your hair and nails
have their independent life
measured in dog-years.

And you are as old as the prophecies
you still have to fulfil,
as old as the riddles
you haven't deciphered,
as old as your dreams.

And you are as old as the dawn
as the shifting summerlight
as the rainswept morning,
as old and as new and as freshlaid
as a baby laughing at fairies.

And you are as old as you feel,
twelve, and twenty-four, and ninety-six,
all jostling together from moment to moment,
seventeen dancing, and forty-five knowing,
and a hundred and three getting out of a bad chair.

And you are sixty this morning,
but you didn't know how to be nine either,
not when you first started,
so you found the words and went on,
because you are as old as your tongue.

May 2011

Nonsense Poem

There's a purpose for metre and rhyme
There's a time for a chapter and verse
There are worse things than cats sat on mats
On the hat of the flat universe.
There's a moment for mentioning June
(And the moon that must always complete her)
It's much neater when love rhymes above
And you don't have to shove out of metre.
When you set out to rhyme with a reason
And the seasoning word comes to you,
The position it lies in 's what makes the word wise 'n,
Emphasizing it, makes it seem true.
Whatever your thoughts as you make rhyme upon it,
at the end of a sonnet, you're on it.

September 2006

"Nemi," "Jane Austen Among the Women," and "When We Were Robots in Egypt" were first published on *Tor.com*.

"After the Spindle" was first published in the Pi.con program book 2011.

"The Weatherkeeper's Diary" was first published in *Stone Telling*.

An Interview with Jo Walton

Conducted by Lynne M. Thomas*

LMT: Tell us a bit about your novel writing process. Is your experience of writing each novel different than the last? You've identified yourself as a "binge" writer in other interviews. How do you cope with the sometimes long spaces between binges? Do you listen to music or draw upon particular images that relate to your novels?

JW: Yes, every novel is different, and just as I teach myself how to write one novel and I think I know how to do it, I have to figure out how to write a different one. *Among Others* has no chapters, and it really messed up my process writing a book with no chapters!

I write in Protext, which is my brain computer interface. I started using it in 1987 in C/PM+, and I joke that I had it fitted as a cyberpunk brain-computer interface. It's an awesome word processor for writing novels. Most word processors think you're interested in writing letters and want you to work in black on white. Protext has a lot of things that make writing novels better and lets me work in grey on black and navy on grey. I've known all the key commands for decades now, and if you ask me what they are my fingers move on their own. My fingers moving on their own is the whole thing, I know my fingers are moving when I'm writing in the same way I know my lungs are moving when I'm breathing, but it's all below my conscious control. I don't still write in CP/M, of course; I upgraded to DOS in 1992 and never looked back. Or forward either... I collect 386 and 486 laptops so that I can keep writing.

I play music while I write, usually Bach. I burn candles, I face west, I have a good chair, I have the apartment to myself with a block of time without interruptions — if I really want to write I can write anywhere using anything. The rest of the time, I try to optimize conditions for me to keep writing. I wrote my novel *Farthing* in 17 days. I always say I write all my books in 17 days, just 17 days spread out over about a year.

Between binges I do research, and I do other things. I find forcing myself to write every day to be supremely counter-productive. However, it can be hard to judge whether I'm just being lazy. I think of it like a tap; sometimes it gushes, sometimes it drips, and sometimes it's dry. I can sometimes get the drip to turn into reasonable flow if I go about it the right way. Generally, writing a poem is a good test. Poems aren't very long, usually, and they're complete then, and I can pretty much always write one. I have written poems to see how my flow is. The other thing that helps is procrastination. I can write much better if I'm avoiding doing something I want to do less. I've got on quite well with my new thing while telling myself I need to do this interview. And if I have to call the accountant my productiveness soars.

LMT: You've mentioned that you're a self-taught writer, and that early in your career you read quite a few books about writing, many of which made you recoil in horror. Is there a particular piece of writing advice that makes you howl with laughter? Are there any bits of advice that you've come to reconsider as more valuable as your writing career has matured and changed?

JW: I think you misunderstood what I said. I tried to read books about writing, and I'd generally read about half a page and get paralyzed and be unable to get on. I really couldn't read them. I've talked about it as being allergic to them, because it was almost like that. I wanted to read them — I wanted to know how to write — but I just couldn't make myself. To this day I think I've only read one whole book on writing, which is Le Guin's *Steering the Craft*.

But bad writing advice — "write what you know." There's a grain of truth here, which is better expressed as "don't write what you don't know." But the way they say it is destructive. The thing everybody could write if they write what they know is what it's like to be thirteen and surrounded by aliens. You know a lot more than is immediately apparent. Oh, and "show don't tell." Showing and telling are tools; sometimes you want one and sometimes the other. And it's all telling! If somebody uses "show don't tell" to mean, "You need to expand this bit, there should be a whole chapter of Sue watering the garden and thinking about Miriam, not just one line," then that's fine, but as general uncontexted advice, it saves people from being terse at the cost of them never being able to skip anything or summarize. And sometimes you really do best saying "Cath was really angry" rather than "Cath's face turned red and she bunched her fists and gritted her teeth and…" It's just as clichéd and longer.

Oh, and that "scene and sequel" thing, where you're supposed to write in a repetitive pattern like that. I never read the book it was from, but I've seen people talk about it online. What a terrible idea!

And "write every day"! No way.

I think there's a tendency to take things that are solutions to particular problems or which work for some people and pronounce them as if they're universal laws. It's as if somebody found that they can paint Caucasian flesh tones by putting green underneath and now they want everyone to put green underneath everything all the time just because.

Oh, and no, I haven't reconsidered any of these things and found them less deadly. My favorite piece of writing advice is Kipling's. "There are nine and sixty ways of constructing tribal lays, and every single one of them is right!" People are different, novels are different, novels are different from shorter things — I just figured out how the other day, incidentally. It's not the length, which is what people always say. It has to do with the weight of the end. The end has to be heavy enough to weigh down what has come before. If it's too heavy it drags the thing off the table; if it's not heavy enough it doesn't hold it down. So a story has to be exactly as long as the weight of the end will hold.

So what I actually did when I was teaching myself to write was that because I literally couldn't read the books (and I didn't live anywhere there were classes and online didn't exist yet) I made up a whole lot of critical terms and ways of looking at writing that don't necessarily make any sense to anyone except me. And I still find them useful.

LMT: Many of your novels focus on the small, the domestic, the personal, individual story as part of a grander world scheme. You often begin telling stories after what would be considered a climax in other novels, focusing on "what happens next." What do you find so interesting about what happens after? What does it tell us about the stories we tell one another that they often overlook the part where life goes on?

JW: I just think it's more interesting. Also it's a way in. You have a huge complicated world, and you can tell the story of somebody who thinks it's ordinary. And then you have a person, a character, who has family and friends and an agenda, and that can take you through. Real life is interesting.

I don't "often" write about what happens next. I did that with *Among Others*, and I've done it with one short story and one poem.

As for what it tells us, I think most people must be more interested in retelling stories than I am, in doing the same thing over and over or reading the variations on themes. I get tired of things. I also think that other people must be much more interested in particular kinds of heroes and heroic things, particular kinds of shapes of story that stop at conventional times. And explosions. I'm not very interested in explosions either.

And I worry about people after the end. I saw the movie *Brassed Off* last night, and I figured out twenty years of detailed happy endings for all the characters, including what universities the kids will go to. It's just a thing I do.

LMT: You mention in interviews that you still run a gaming group. Tell us about your life as a gamer. What kinds of games do you prefer? How does gaming influence your writing?

JW: I think gaming influenced my writing in that it let me believe that I could write a long thing and have the plot work without needing to work it all out in detail in advance, which kills my interest in actually writing it. I ran an Everway game for an academic year in which I let the players do exactly what they wanted, and then at the end it was all one perfect thing. I thought that if I could do that, I could do it with a novel where I could go back and change things and fix things and I was in charge of the characters. It gave me confidence.

I generally run Everway for fantasy and pick-up games and GURPS for science fiction. My gaming group is a fairly typical post-college group — two generations of two families, four women, two men, two published genre writers, ages from 12 through 55. I'm running a kind of Cherryh-esque space adventure with smuggling and aliens and space stations. We play once a fortnight on a Friday.

I prefer the kind of game that has good characters and lots of actual roleplaying. Sometimes we don't touch dice or look at figures for weeks.

LMT: You were born in Wales and now live in Canada. The experience of growing up and living much of your life in the UK has clearly influenced your work (*Tooth and Claw*, the Small Change Trilogy, *Among Others*, for example). Has moving to Quebec affected your writing?

JW: I think it's too soon to tell yet. I expect it will, but it takes things time to trickle through.

LMT: One of my favorite parts of *Tooth and Claw* is how well you reproduce the pacing and timbre of a Trollope novel while still not breaking the frame of the characters all being played by dragons. What was more challenging: producing a novel that felt as though it was written in the 19th century, or integrating the dragon aspects into that setting?

JW: The two things were both integral. Actually, both of those things were really fun. I'm trying to remember what was difficult about *T&C*—some of the dragon details. The hats, and the material culture, getting that integrated at the right level. I was so pleased when I realized they traveled long distances on open carriages of trains but rose up to fly for a bit and then settle back, that was just right.

LMT: The Small Change Trilogy (*Farthing, Ha'Penny, Half a Crown*) posits a world in which England worked to appease Germany rather than fighting the Second World War. All three use murder mystery and thriller tropes to explore an alternate historical timeline, while focusing on small, personal stories at their core. What drew you to this particular setting for alternate history?

JW: Actually they fought WWII from September 1939 to May 1941 and then called it a draw because they got the Hess peace offer and realized they couldn't possibly win. Which they couldn't—even with the US and the USSR it was a close thing, and without them and with no sign of either of them coming in it would have been impossible. In reality both of them only joined WWII because they were attacked, and nobody could count on the Axis powers being so very reckless.

There's a way in which people think of history as being inevitable and don't realize they're living in history right now, making history every day with their choices. I've always found alternate history fascinating, because there are so many change points where everything could have been completely different.

I thought of the Small Change history when I was reading Josephine Tey's *Brat Farrar* and wondered what year it was supposed to be set in. There are all these things that happened ten years ago in France, and the book was published in 1952, and no British people were going on holiday in France in our 1942. And I'd thought before that anybody who wasn't Churchill would have given up and made peace in 1941, and so I started reading *Brat Farrar* and thinking that Hitler was at the Channel and nobody cared, and here were all these smug upper-class people worrying about their horses and inheritances when the Holocaust was going on. This was a chilling experience, and I wrote *Farthing* to share it with my friends.

LMT: You've mentioned that *Lifelode* was one of the most difficult novels for you to write and that it didn't quite work for you. What made its process so much more challenging for you? In hindsight, are there things about that novel that you would change?

JW: Gosh, everything. *Lifelode* is a very complex world, in which I was trying to tell a story that went against the grain of fantasy stories, and in as very odd style, which I took from Rumer Godden's *China Court*, because I read *China Court* immediately after *Tehanu* and thought that Godden was doing the women's story that Le Guin wanted to do and couldn't. Of course, I couldn't either, because it's really hard. Who knew?

Some people really like *Lifelode*. I am not one of them.

LMT: You've noted in other interviews that *Among Others* mythologizes part of your experience as a teen, from reading and enjoying classic SF to living with disability. What was the most challenging part of the novel to write? What came the most easily?

JW: The hard part was writing what I know.

It was my life, but it was thirty years ago, I had some detachment. But still I was writing about myself, and that was difficult. I actually wimped out on writing about the accident where my sister was killed. I knew the shape of the scene I needed to write for the way the book was going, and I couldn't make myself write it. Also, if it had been all made up I'd have characterized the evil mother better. And writing the end was hard, because there was no analogy. In real life I never defeated my evil mother, so I had to make that up. Everything else has some basis in reality.

What was easiest was the magic system. I loved doing the magic, the plausibly deniable magic, and the fairies who don't use nouns. I loved calling them fairies, and it makes me laugh when reviewers spell that "faeries" or call them spirits. You might just as well call them aliens! She doesn't know what they are, and she wasn't grown up when she first saw them and she's using this baby word — I like that.

LMT: *Among Others* is, as you've noted, a love letter to fandom. Do you have a particular anecdote that illustrates your personal fandom experiences, and why fans are so important to you?

JW: On my first day in fandom, on the Friday evening of Follycon in 1988, I went out to dinner with John Brunner and Colin Greenland and a couple of fairly big name British fans, because they invited me along with the person who had taken me to the con. We went to a Greek restaurant and we talked about SF, and it was just wonderful. I was twenty-two.

And this year at the pre-Hugo Reception I started chatting with somebody and she explained that she had met James Bacon, who was one of the Hugo nominees for fan writer, and he's asked her to go to the Hugos with him. So she was sitting there chatting with me and George R.R. Martin, and she was twenty-one, and it was her first convention. That's fandom. Still there, still magical, still full of great conversation.

LMT: Why are you drawn to WisCon in particular?

JW: Debbie Notkin is such an amazingly cool person, and she's one of the founders. And some of my friends go every year and talk about having a good time. It has never worked out for me to get there — Madison isn't on Amtrak, and I tend to travel to cons by Amtrak, but I'm delighted to be going this year.

LMT: You originated International Pixel-Stained Technopeasant Day, when professional writers post professional work free to the web, on Shakespeare's birthday, April 23, in 2007. This was a response to comments by Howard Hendrix about how writers posting their work to the web for free devalued the "noble" writing profession. How do you think this annual protest has influenced the field, and what do you have planned for the next one?

JW: Howard Hendrix called people posting their work online for free "scabs." I'm from the South Wales Valleys, and to me that's a real fighting word; it's one of the worst things you can call anyone.

I'm not a huge fanatic about posting work online for free. I don't care all that much about it. Do it if you want, don't if you don't want. But heck, it's not being a scab if you do.

I post poetry online all the time — all the time. I can get $5 for a poem, and I can usually get $5 for a poem I've already posted on my livejournal. And $5 is not worth as much to me as the instant gratification of having feedback.

So Hendrix was vice president of SFWA, and he said these amazingly incendiary things, and he irritated me. I was nominated for a Nebula at the time, for Farthing, although I wasn't a member of SFWA. (I'm still not.) But I thought it gave me some standing to oppose that — and I didn't think about it all that much. I just posted on my journal that I was declaring it International Pixel-Stained Technopeasant day and that people should post stuff online for free. I wasn't expecting the overwhelming response I got — I thought maybe some of my friends would do it. I was going to say it was that day, but one of my friends said he needed to format something and I should announce it for next week, and I saw that a week later was

Shakespeare's birthday and that seemed appropriate. I was amazed at the response.

I haven't done anything much to keep it up since or celebrate it every year. I think it made its point — posting stuff online is a legitimate choice; it doesn't make you a scab. I don't think it's influenced the field, especially, though maybe seeing that this huge number of professional writers thought posting stuff online was OK did change the perception of that. I don't know.

LMT: Do you consider yourself to be a feminist? How have your politics influenced your writing, and vice versa?

JW: Of course I'm a feminist.

I think politics in writing is like salt in ice-cream — you want it on the outside making things cold, not on the inside making things salty. My politics influences everything because the person I am influences everything.

LMT: Tell us about a story that shook you to your core. What about it caused it to resonate so deeply with you?

JW: Abu Ghraib. Those smiling faces in the photographs. It made me realize I'd become complacent about the Holocaust. I knew about it; it couldn't come at me around a blind corner any more. But there were those smiling home photos of torturers, and they weren't monsters, they were people. Smiling. And one of them was a woman.

LMT: Do you have any guilty pleasures? Are there stories (tv series, films, comics, gaming worlds, books) that you absolutely adore, but you think that your fans would find your love for them a bit…unusual?

JW: I think guilt about food and culture and art is deeply misplaced.

There are some things I like that you might think would surprise people, but I've mostly written about them. W.E.B. Griffin sits next to Nicola Griffith on my bookshelves, and H. Beam Piper next to Marge Piercy, with Plato between her and Jerry Pournelle. I've always thought that would make a wonderful ideal convention panel, but you'd need a great moderator. I like some romance—Jennifer Crusie, Lani Diane Rich, Georgette Heyer. I read a lot of chick lit last summer because I was trying to figure it out as a genre. Daniel Abraham had this great post about genre being where fears pool, and I wondered what fear was pooling there—I think it has to do with getting older and being successful in a career and having partners but no commitment. So that was interesting, and I enjoyed that.

I don't like TV for the most part, and I don't like genre movies—see "explosions" above. I like good acting. I love live theatre. We go to a lot of live theatre, and sometimes it's not all that good, but I don't feel guilty about it.

LMT: What are you working on now? Can you tell us about some upcoming projects?

JW: I have a collection of my Tor.com pieces coming out in January next year, called *What Makes This Book So Great*. That'll be my next actual publication.

I don't want to talk about what I'm writing in case I jinx it, I'm not far on enough to be confident about that, though I should be done by WisCon all being well.

I'm doing research for a fantasy about the Congress of Vienna, and also for a generation starship novel, which is going really slowly because SF is hard.

---

*[Special thanks to Maggie Slater and Sarah Monette for their invaluable advice. –LMT]

Author Biographies

Jo Walton
has run out of eggs and needs to go buy some,
she has no time to write a bio
as she wants to make spanakopita today.
She also wants to write a new chapter
and fix the last one.
Oh yes, she writes stuff,
when people leave her alone to get on with it
and don't demand bios
and proofreading and interviews
and dinner.
Despite constant interruptions
she has published nine novels
in the last forty-eight years
and started lots of others.
She won the Campbell for Best New Writer in 2002
when she was 38.
She has also written half a ton of poetry
which isn't surprising as she finds poetry
considerably easier to write
than short bios listing her accomplishments.
She is married, with one (grown up, awesome) son
who lives nearby with his girlfriend and two cats.
She also has lots of friends
who live all over the planet
who she doesn't see often enough.
She remains confused by punctuation,
"who" and "whom"
and "that" and "which."

She cannot sing and has trouble with arithmetic
also, despite living ten years in Montreal
her French still sucks.
Nevertheless, her novel *Among Others*
won a Hugo and a Nebula
so she must be doing something right
at least way back when she wrote it
it'll probably never work again.
She also won a World Fantasy Award in 2004
for an odd book called *Tooth and Claw*
in which everyone is dragons.
She comes from South Wales
and identifies ethnically
as a Romano-Briton
but she emigrated to Canada
because it seemed a better place
to stand to build the future.
She blogs about old books on Tor.com
and posts poetry and recipes and wordcount on her LJ
and is trying to find something to bribe herself with
as a reward for writing a bio
that isn't chocolate.

Joan Slonczewski was the first woman to win a Campbell Award (*A Door into Ocean*, 1986), and the only author since Fred Pohl to win a second Campbell (*The Highest Frontier*, 2011). A microbiologist, she writes hard science fiction about women of color as scientists, and explores diverse sexualities. *The Highest Frontier* depicts a Cuban-American woman going to college in a space habitat. Frontera College is run by a male couple, while on Earth a lesbian is running for president. Slonczewski's award-winning classic, *A Door into Ocean* creates a world covered entirely by ocean, inhabited by an all-female race of purple people who use genetic engineering and nonviolent resistance to defend their unique ecosystem. *Brain Plague* (2000) depicts intelligent alien microbes that invade our brains. The secret of these unique addictive microbes is discovered by a human-gorilla woman scientist in *The Children Star* (1998). Slonczewski's books show a pansexual perspective, including human-ape hybrids and humans married to intelligent machines. Her early work was inspired by the works of Ursula Le Guin, Octavia Butler, Anne McCaffrey, and Tanith Lee. Slonczewski teaches biology at Kenyon College, including the notorious course "Biology in Science Fiction."